Copyright © 2022 by Emily Dreeling
All rights reserved. This book or any portion thereof
may not be reproduced or used in any manner whatsoever
without the express written permission of the publisher
except for the use of brief quotations in a book review.

ISBN 979-8-9853105-4-2

This book is dedicated to
the bestest friend and watchdog
that there ever was,
Murphy

River

and the Missing Yellow Wellie Mystery

written by
Emily Dreeling

illustrated by
Misha Jovanovic

Sunrise, and as light begins
to flood the hallway, Bertie, Lexie,
and Miley, who are just waking up,
discover that their best friend Teddy is
no longer beside them on the shoe rack.

"Hmm," says Miley, "that's strange!
I could have sworn River put us all back
in our usual places when we came in from
the garden yesterday."

"Well, maybe she was up early and took
Teddy out again," suggests Lexie.

"EARLIER?!" shrieks Bertie.
"IT'S ONLY DAWN!"

"Exactly," says Miley. "I think we should start looking for him, because he always makes such a fuss getting up and none of us heard a thing!"

"That's true," nods Lexie. "He's a total grump first thing in the morning, huffing and puffing till we're all awake!

"Ok, here's what we'll do. Miley, can you sneak upstairs to see if River's still in bed? And Bertie, can you quickly check the backyard from the dog flap? I think I should stay put, just in case he comes back in the meantime."

"Great plan!" whoops Miley.

"YES, nice one Lexie!" says Bertie.
"Righto then, let's get a move on Miley,
we need to get this search underway!"

Moments later the crew meet back
in the hall and discuss their findings.

"Well, he didn't show up while you were gone,"
says Lexie disappointedly. "Did you two have any luck?"

"So, River's still fast asleep," says Miley.

"And there's not a soul in the garden," adds Bertie, with a look of sheer terror beginning to cross his face.

"Whoa, Bertie, what's wrong?" asks Lexie.

"Oh jeez, oh no, oh jeez, oh no...," he replies, repeating himself over and over frantically.

"Ehh, you're kinda freaking us out here Bertie! For real, stop ranting and tell us WHAT'S UP?!" demands Miley.

"Oh jeez, okay, oh jeez...well, it's just that, well, I've just remembered that Murphy's basket was empty when I snuck past it to look through the flap..."

Immediately understanding Bertie's panic,
the gang are thrown into a spin when they realize
River's naughty little pup may have kidnapped
Teddy in the middle of the night.

"Crikey, this looks bad for sure," says Lexie, trembling.

"Yes, it does," agrees Miley, who was now pacing the
floor in circles behind a near hysterical Bertie.

"Okay everyone, WE NEED TO THINK!" she exclaims,
finally coming to a halt. "The only way Teddy could have
possibly been taken by Murphy is if he wasn't placed back
on the rack properly. He'll only target what's lying around,
so can anyone definitely recall seeing him beside us before
the lights went out?!"

"No," groans Lexie. "I was so tired after all the running and jumping about we did that I passed out straight away."

"Oh jeez, me too!" cries Bertie, holding his head in his hands. "So heaven knows what Murphy's probably done to him. That old rogue is capable of anything!"

"Too right! He's seriously out of control, and River doesn't seem to get how important it is that we're not left strewn about!" says Miley.

"Hey, it's not River's fault he's such a scoundrel!" chides Lexie.

"Oh gosh, I'm sorry," she answers. "I know she loves us, and that she'll be just as upset when she finds out Teddy's gone."

"FOR GOOOOOD...," warbles a choked up Bertie, and with that all three begin to cry.

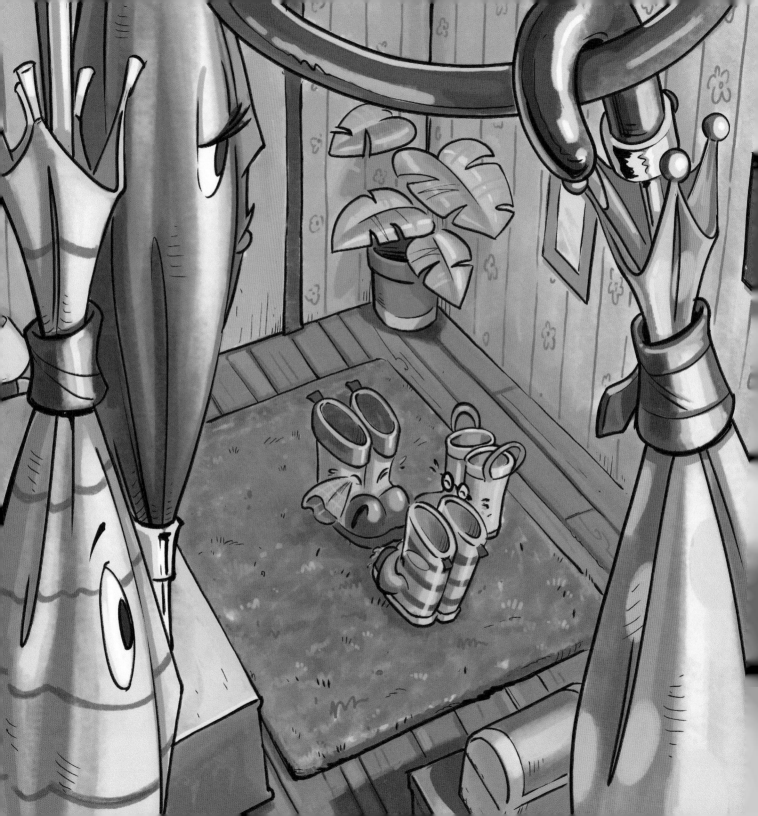

Overhead on the coat hanger,
Pearl, Polly, and Priscilla, have
been woken by the wails of the distraught
little wellies below. And upon hearing the
news of Teddy's disappearance, can't wait
to chime in on the unfolding disaster.

"Suffering ducks! So that barking mad brat's
at it again, eh?!" says Pearl to the weeping trio.

"Has to be the case," says Polly, quickly
cutting in. "Because if there's no sign of either
of them, it can only mean ONE thing..."

"Yup, DAISIES! Teddy's pushing them up
right now for certain," concludes Priscilla.
"Shame that, such a lovely lad..."

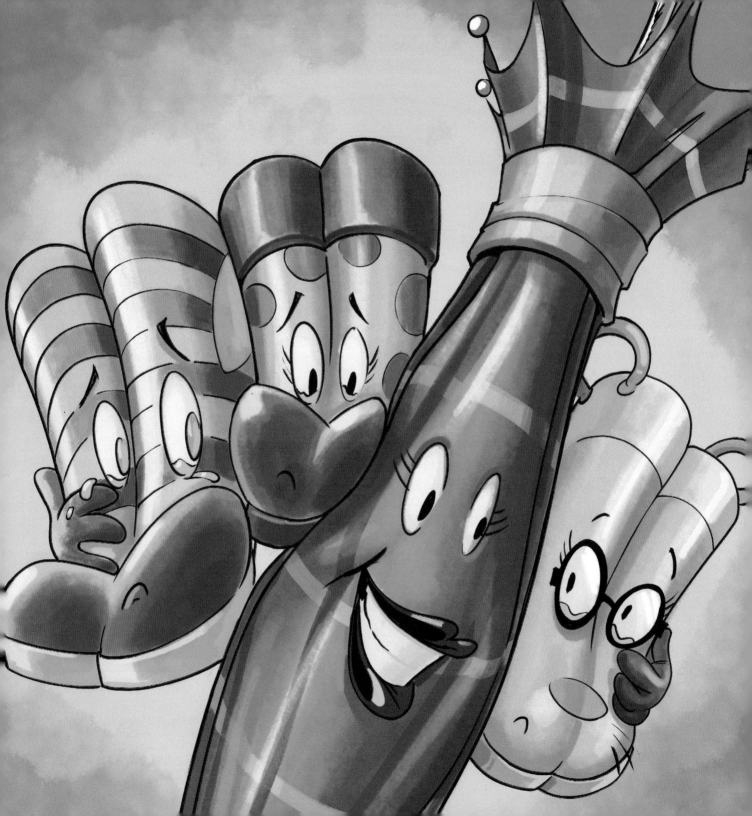

"Here we go! Adding one plus
one and coming up with three,
AS, PER, USUAL!" snorts Trudy.

"I've said it before and I'll say it
again kids, ignore those miserable old hags
up there! They've already written Teddy off,
and while I admit it's suspect, we need to collect
our facts FIRST before getting carried away..."

"FACTS?!" snaps Pearl. "The FACTS are that
Murphy's bad behavior is well-known around
these parts. For heaven's sake, there's not a
loose glove, scarf, or shoe of any kind
safe with him about the place!"

"AN ABSOLUTE TERROR!" says Polly, continuing the rant. "I'll never forget what he did to old Peggy. One half of her never found, and the other half...UGH, it was truly awful! She was COMPLETELY MANGLED!"

"A pure and utter NIGHTMARE!" adds Priscilla, gasping at the memory. "Heels flapping and toes like Swiss cheese! It seemed she tried to stay rooted to the spot to save herself, but by the looks of things, the more she resisted, the worse it was for her!"

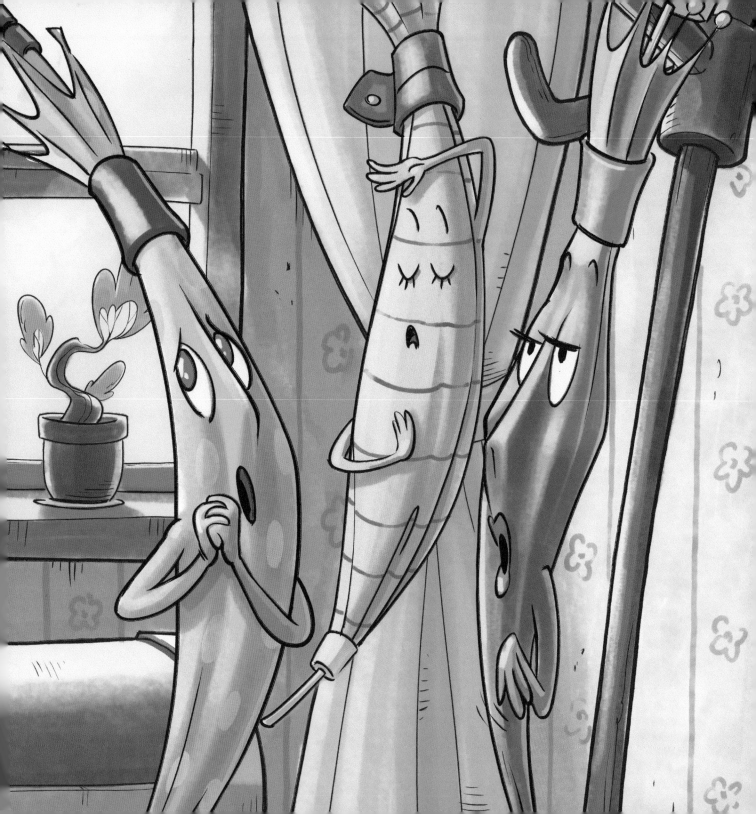

Being too young to remember this particular tragedy, Bertie, Lexie, and Miley, are now beside themselves thinking about the horror that may have befallen their friend.

"I can't imagine how frightened Teddy must have been," snuffles Bertie. "Everyone knows he's just a big scaredy-cat behind it all. I just wish we were there to help him..."

"As I mentioned before being RUDELY interrupted, it's high time we gathered some proper evidence here. You're all going crazy, even though we're not sure a crime has ACTUALLY been committed!" says Trudy, throwing a side-eye towards the coat hanger. So calm down wee one's, this case isn't closed just yet!"

"You're right," says Lexie. "We've got to pull ourselves together! There may still be time to find him. And if we're lucky, maybe before River gets up too!"

"Luck?!" says Miley. "We'll need some kind of mastermind to sort this one out... OH WAIT! I KNOW! There's Detective Walter! We forgot all about him!"

"YES! THAT'S IT! We should head over to Grotland Yard and see if he can help us out!" says Lexie.

"Brilliant!" says Bertie, beginning to brighten up. "Walter's a bit of a legend by all accounts, so maybe there's hope after all!"

"That's the spirit!" cheers Trudy. "Never forget, there's ALWAYS hope! And Grotland is a wonderful place to start figuring out the truth behind this whole mess!"

"YAY!" shout the threesome, and after thanking Trudy for her encouragement, Lexie shoo's Bertie and Miley towards the back door.

Carefully tiptoeing their
way towards the Yard, Lexie takes
the lead, covering Bertie and Miley.
A short time later they safely reach the
station, and everybody thanks their lucky
stars that they haven't run into
Murphy along the way.

Knocking the door, a gruff voice inside asks them for the secret password to enter. Knowing they don't have it, Lexie - turning to ask the others what they should do - discovers they've been gatecrashed.

"BOO!" yells River at the top of her lungs. "Bet y'all didn't expect to see me, HUH?!"

Horrified, Bertie screeches and faints. Miley begins fanning him, while puffing wildly into a brown paper bag herself.

"But, but, but...the magic mud dust...," she stutters, after catching her breath.

"Darn!" says Lexie. "It mustn't have worked this time!"

"You don't say!" snips Miley.

Just then Bertie starts coming around.
"Oh jeez, so this wasn't all a bad dream...,"
he says, rubbing his eyes furiously.

"NOPE!" replies River. "So, WAKEY-WAKEY!
The sooner we find Teddy the better, because
something's not right. He's gone, even though
I made sure to rack him properly
before I went upstairs."

Scrambling to his feet and
scratching his head, Bertie peers in Lexie's
direction. "But how? How did the dust have no
effect? I thought the elders said if we sprinkled
it over her every night she'd never find out
we were real!"

"They did!" says Lexie, recalling the instructions Wilhelmina, Nellie, and Stella, gave them to protect their secret. "I've been doing it ever since our trip to see them on Galoshes Mountain and there hasn't been a problem, until now..."

Suddenly, a flashback of the previous evening pops into her head.

"So, umm, I think I may have an inkling what happened. I think it didn't work because, ehh... I kinda forgot to do it last night..."

Bertie and Miley both stare in disbelief.

"HEY, don't look at me like that! It was SO way past our bedtime, it wasn't even funny. I just conked out, okay?! Sorryyyyy..."

"Listen," says River, "I don't know what this magic dust is that you're so fussed about, but it can't be that special because it seems like no amount of it will ever change the fact that you're all as real to me as I am to you!

"Anyways, we really need to shake a leg and find Teddy as quickly as we can. Time is ticking, and I want to be back in bed before Mom finds me out here talking to my shoes.

"She's already worried I've got too many 'imaginary friends', and I don't want her thinking there's four more to add to the list. So you can save your mud sprinkles, because I'm never EVER letting the cat out the bag!"

Bertie and Miley start breakdancing.

"I think it's safe to say that's a HUGE weight
off our minds!" says Lexie, laughing at the pair's antics.
"But while we're on the subject of cats in sticky situations,
at this stage we'll have to guess the password if
we're to have any chance of getting
Teddy out of the bind he's in!"

"Hmm... why don't we try 'man cave'?" suggests River.
"That's what Dad always calls it, so maybe it's worth a shot?"

"Perfect!" replies Lexie. "That'll get the ball rolling!
Okay Walter, it's 'MAN CAVE'!" she roars through
the peephole.

"BINGO!" he hurls back. "Come on in!"

Amazed they hit the jackpot on their first try,
they waste no time piling into Grotland behind her.

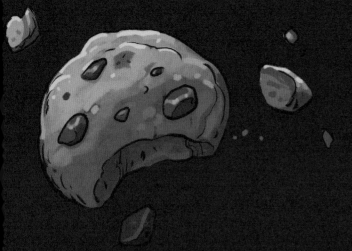

Inside, Grotland Yard is in full swing.
Walter is barely visible behind a sea of empty
packets of biscuits, and stacks upon stacks of
files on his workbench. Poring over the details
of his latest case, he is delighted by the
excuse their interruption gives him
for a tea break.

"Ah, wee booties, what can I do for you today? And I see you've brought some company? Ronnie, on with the kettle!"

Hastily introducing River, Lexie then relays the unfortunate events of the morning to him.

"Blimey! There hasn't been a crisis of this sort since old Peggy's disappearance a couple of years back. Awful business it was, and we certainly don't want a repeat! So first things first, I'll need a detailed description of the victim. Ronnie, fetch me a fresh notepad on the double!"

"Okay, just to recap – stripy, no front teeth, and about the same height as you three – GOT IT!" says Walter, after carefully reviewing the information given to him by the crew.

"Ronnie, you've already been through the lost and found box this morning. Did you see anything matching these particulars?"

Ronnie blinks twice.

"Heh, thought not," sighs Walter. "Righto, then I suggest we each take a section of the premises and search it high and low."

"YES! Let's go!" says Lexie eagerly.
"Bertie, why don't you take upstairs,
while Miley looks downstairs, and River,
if you could check the garage?"

"Excellent strategy Lexie," Walter chips in.
"And I can inspect the backyard, while you
examine the front. We'll meet back here in
a half hour with our updates.

"Oh, one more thing...Ronnie, fetch the
walkie-talkies, there's a good lad!"

Ronnie blinks once, then scarpers.

"So we can reach one another if there's an emergency,"
explains Walter, taking the radios from Ronnie and
passing them out.

"Okay Ronnie, it's your turn to man the fort. I know it's more than safe in your capable hands!"

Ronnie blinks once, then standing to attention, mirrors Walter's salute.

Behind them in the doorway, River and the trio struggle to contain their laughter until Walter turns to address them.

"Troops, it's time to turn this place UPSIDE DOWN!"

To their surprise, they suddenly straighten up and salute him too as he strides purposefully past them into the garden.

Immediately splitting once outside, they scour every nook and cranny of the house and yard.

The thirty minutes fly by, and when their time is up, Walter calls everyone back to base.

Arriving back at the shed,
Ronnie is told to make another pot of
tea. A few minutes later, the worn-out gang
are served a fresh brew and some biscuits.
Rolling out a map of the grounds
on the table in front of them,
Walter begins to study it.

"Well, I'm stumped!" he mumbles,
through a mouthful of cookies.
"Every corner and crevice
combed, and ZILCH!"

Everybody looks beyond glum,
and as Bertie pulls a hanky out to mop up
the stream of tears now running down his cheeks,
he accidentally brushes aside a few crumbs that had
been covering River's treehouse.

"At least in old Peg's case there was some bit of a
sole left to go on!" continues Walter. "But this?!
Not so much as a stray bootstrap for a clue!

"My friends, I'm afraid there's nothing else for it
but to close the file altogether. Ronnie, I know it'll be
tight, but can you try and squeeze it into the completely
unsolvable mysteries cabinet over there once you've
boiled the kettle..."

"HANG ON!" exclaims Miley, noticing the
displaced morsels. "The TREEHOUSE! Has anyone
checked the TREEHOUSE?!"

Realizing he's missed a key part of his search area, Walter's face begins to redden.

"But, of course! How on earth did THAT fall through the cracks?!" says Lexie, giving him a side-eye.

"Alright, c'mon everyone!" she whoops, jumping down from the table. "This is our last hope, but if he's not out here, I'll eat my right wellie!"

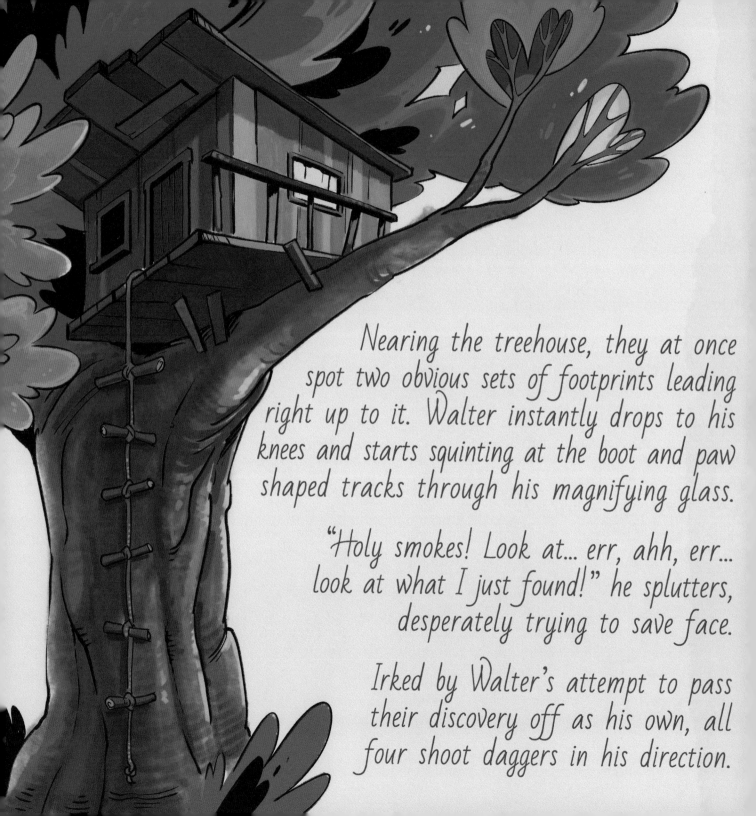

Nearing the treehouse, they at once spot two obvious sets of footprints leading right up to it. Walter instantly drops to his knees and starts squinting at the boot and paw shaped tracks through his magnifying glass.

"Holy smokes! Look at... err, ahh, err... look at what I just found!" he splutters, desperately trying to save face.

Irked by Walter's attempt to pass their discovery off as his own, all four shoot daggers in his direction.

With his detective skills now in question, Lexie decides she'd better take charge and is first up the ladder. River, Miley and Bertie follow, then Walter is last, panting heavily as he tries to keep up with the young ones.

As they reach the top, their jaws drop one by one as they try to take in the scene before them.

All are lost for words until Walter appears and sees the missing pair having breakfast together.

"Well, I'll be darned! In all my years I never thought I'd see a cat and dog become friends, let alone breaking bread!"

Startled by Walter's voice, Teddy and Murphy's jaws hit the floor too.

Gathering herself, River runs straight over to Teddy and locks him in an airtight embrace.

"Oh Teddy, my old buddy, my old pal, YOU'RE ALIVE!" she cries, squeezing him senseless. "And I know you're REAL and stuff too! Lexie forgot to sprinkle me last night, so you don't have to pretend anymore! Say something! PLEASE! Did you miss me loads as well?!"

Prizing a hand free, Teddy gives Lexie a big thumbs up.

Seconds later, a loud thud prompts
River to let him go. Discovering Bertie has
collapsed at the mere sight of Murphy, her relief
at finding the duo quickly fades when she realizes
he might be holding Teddy hostage.

"Say, Murphy, what exactly is going
on here, hmm?" she says.

"AHEM, ah yes, what exactly is going on?!"
echoes Walter, sensing his services may not be needed
much longer. Rattled by the thought of his reputation
in tatters, he whips out a pair of handcuffs to haul
off Murphy in a last ditch attempt to look useful.

"WHOA! Hang on a minute!" says River,
leaping in front of him to stop the arrest.
"Let's give him a chance to explain first."

Too embarrassed to tell the truth,
Murphy tries to change the subject.

"SO, anyone fancy a cuppa? Maybe
some freshly squeezed juice?"

Keen to hear his confession, everyone but Walter
says no. Then seeing the highly annoyed look on
the search party's faces, he politely declines.

"Look, I've got to be back in bed pretty soon, so quit
stalling Murphy, SPILL!" says River impatiently.

"Oh alright, alright!" he grumps. "Well, for starters, Teddy
isn't being held here against his will. I'm well aware of what
you all think of me, and that's the very reason why
I asked for his help a few weeks back."

"You see, I want to mend my wellie-ripping ways, and thought he'd be the perfect candidate to teach this old dog some new tricks. Given he's a tough guy too, but with lots of friends, I wanted to know his secret.

"I thought convincing him would be tricky with my track record, but it was easy once I figured out he was really a huge fraidy-cat. I knew because he took off running when I first tried to pin him down for a meeting, so I was quite sure once I finally caught up with him that we could make a deal.

"Luckily, I was right on the money – he was in need of some pointers too! So, we agreed, that he'd show me how to be a bit kinder, and I'd show him how to be a bit braver. And the rest, as they say, is history."

"Be the hokey!" chuckles Walter. "So that's why the crime rates have been down with the last while!"

"Just as well," whispers Miley to the others, "since his right boot doesn't know what his left is doing!"

After a fit of giggles, all eyes turn to Teddy, and River asks him if Murphy is indeed being honest.

"Yes, it's all true!" beams Teddy.
"And we've learned an awful lot from each other during these morning chats.

"Murphy's taught me that it's okay to be scared, but that I must try to slowly but surely conquer each of my fears so they can't get ahold of me like they do.

"I think I'll always be timid at heart, but his advice will help me feel much more courageous in those moments when I'm most afraid."

Blushing, Murphy continues their unlikely tale.

"And Teddy has taught me that although it's normal to be angry every now and then, like fear, you mustn't let it get a grip of you. So every time I'm cross I must take some time-out, and some deep breaths, to help me stay calm."

Flabbergasted, River is the first
of the rescue team to speak.

"WOW! What a journey you've both been on.
It sounds like you're a changed pup, Murphy?!"

"Erm, well, I'm fairly sure all wellies on home
turf are out of danger for now," he replies.

Bertie, Lexie, and Miley, all breathe a sigh
of relief. "BUT," he drools, "I can't say the
same for those three weather-beaten
old brollies inside."

Still on high alert, Walter whips his handcuffs out again, but this time it's Teddy that steps in to save Murphy.

"Oh, calm down Walter! We're covering umbrellas next week, then walking sticks the week after. This is going to take some time, you know?! He's still very much a work in progress!"

Disappointed, Walter shoves them back in his coat pocket.

"Oh Teddy, I'm so proud of you!" says River. "I know you've got some ground left to cover with Murphy, but what an amazing job you've done already!"

"You can chalk that one down!" nods Lexie. "He's come on leaps and bounds! So much so I think it's safe enough to officially welcome him to the gang! I mean, if that's okay with everyone?"

"Fine by me!" says Bertie. "Any pal of Teddy's is a pal of ours! And if you decide to become part of the group Murphy, then we can ALL help you out of the pickle you're in!"

"Absolutely!" agrees Miley. "After all, a trouble shared is a trouble halved. Hmm... but in this instance there's five of us, so your worries would only ever be teeny-weeny. Heck, from a numbers point of view you'd be mad to turn us down! So, whaddya say Murphy? YOU IN?!"

"YOU BETCHA!" he answers, welling up.
"I can't tell you how much your kindness
means to me! And I promise, in return for
seeing me through this rough patch, I'm going
to be the bestest friend and watchdog
to you all that there is!"

"YAY!" shouts River. "All my
buddies getting along together is just
a dream come true!"

Everybody jumps up and down excitedly,
except Walter, who has tiptoed towards
the exit having seen the floor sway beneath.

Trying to gauge how much longer they've got before
the boards give way, he checks his watch, only to find
there's a more pressing concern.

"Cripes! It looks like this investigation
has been wrapped just in time. River,
you've less than five minutes to get
into bed! And you four, you must
get yourselves back on the
shoe rack, NOW!"

"*EEK!*" squeaks River.
"We'll NEVER make it!"

"*YES WE WILL!*" declares Lexie. "Murphy, can
you distract River's folks somehow till we're all
back where we're supposed to be?"

"Consider it done!" he responds, without missing
a beat. "A suspect wet patch on their bedroom carpet
should do the trick! Let me run on ahead."

The whole crew cheer as he bounds down
the steps immediately.

River, Lexie, Miley, and Teddy quickly follow,
with each one thanking Walter for his help as
they hop out the door.

"My pleasure little ones! I'm here anytime you
need a hand. Oh Bertie, just before you go, would you
mind giving out a few of these business cards around
the hallway? Folks are always coming and going down
there, and most don't know about the valuable services
we offer at the Yard!"

In a flurry to catch up with the rest,
Bertie grabs a fistful of them and skips
down the ladder.

Once inside, River and the little brigade laugh as they read the card aloud...

Detective **Walter Wellie's** the name,
And solving mysteries is my game,
So if you're wanting to know who's to blame,
Come out to the yard, you'll be glad you came!

In case of emergency, please call
1-800-GROT

P.S. Tea and biscuits are
on the house, but please don't
forget to tip young Ronnie!

"You know, this morning has proved that we're more than capable of figuring things out by ourselves. So, thankfully, we won't be needing him to crack any cases for us in the near future!" says Lexie proudly.

"That's for sure!" chirps River. "But I think it'd be nice to pop in and just say hello every now and again. Walter's a hoot of a boot, and that Ronnie really makes a mean cuppa!"

Everyone nods in agreement.

"Okay, time to split!" says River, seeing the clock just about to strike eight. "I'll catch y'all after breakfast, okay?!"

She disappears upstairs in a flash while the four zip back to the rack, ready to get some well-earned rest for a full day of fun and games ahead.

...The End

Printed in Great Britain
by Amazon

30098288R00057